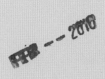

For Anna and Joseph – *P.S.*
For Tony – *A.L.V.*

In the Dark of the Night copyright © Frances Lincoln Limited 2008
Text copyright © Paul Stewart 2008
The right of Paul Stewart to be identified as the author of this work
has been asserted by him in accordance with the Copyright,
Designs and Patents Act, 1988 (United Kingdom).
Illustrations copyright © Tim Vyner 2008

First published in Great Britain in 2008 and the USA in 2009 by
Frances Lincoln Children's Books, 4 Torriano Mews,
Torriano Avenue, London NW5 2RZ
www.franceslincoln.com

British Library Cataloguing in Publication Data
available on request

ISBN: 978-1-84507-764-8

Illustrated with watercolours
Set in Hiroshige

Printed in China
1 3 5 7 9 8 6 4 2

In the Dark
of the Night

Paul Stewart

Illustrated by Tim Vyner

F

FRANCES LINCOLN
CHILDREN'S BOOKS

Papa Wolf! Papa Wolf!
Where are you going, Papa Wolf?

Is that you, Cub-of-Mine?
Are you still not asleep?

I have tried, Papa Wolf. But something inside
will not let me sleep.

Then the time has arrived, Cub-of-Mine.
Get up and make ready to go.

Do I have to get up? Do I have to go out, Papa Wolf?
Why must we leave the snug of the den?

We are going to a special place, Cub-of-Mine – a place
where all the big wolves go. You, too, are big enough now.

It's DARK, Papa Wolf. Why has the sun gone away?
Maybe I am not so big after all...

The sun is asleep, Cub-of-Mine, that is all.
This is the dark of the night.

What are those lights that glinter like teeth, Papa Wolf?
They are making me feel even smaller.

They are stars, Cub-of-Mine.
They show us the way.

And look, Papa Wolf! There are eyes in the trees,
big yellow eyes – and they're staring at me!

They are only the night-birds and rabbits and deer, Cub-of-Mine.
Tonight we shall leave them in peace.

Stop, Papa Wolf! There is an enormous MONSTER!
Papa Wolf! Don't leave me behind.

Be still, Cub-of-Mine. It is nothing but shadows and mist.
Step lightly, and try to keep up.

I'm tired, Papa Wolf.
How much higher do we have to climb?

To the top of the world, Cub-of-Mine – but be strong.
The end of our journey is near.

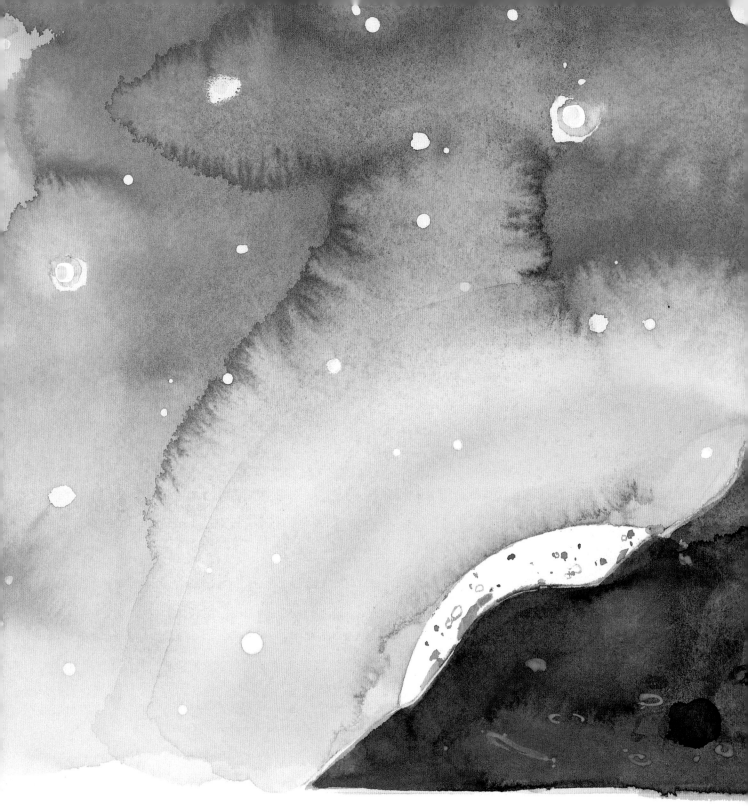

Why have we stopped, Papa Wolf?
What is this place in the mountains?

This is Singing Rock, Cub-of-Mine,
where wolves have always come.

There's a light, Papa Wolf, a silvery light!

That, Cub-of-Mine, is...

...*the Moon.*

It's so bright, Papa Wolf! So big... So white...

And when wolves sing their song together,
it lightens the dark of the night, Cub-of-Mine.
It sends the darkness away.

Song, Papa Wolf? But I don't know the words or the tune.

The song is inside you, Cub-of-Mine. Lift up your head.
Look at the moon. Open your mouth – and sing!

But our songs were exactly the same, Papa Wolf.
Was I copying you? Were you copying me?

I sang from my heart as all wolves do.
We sing, Cub-of-Mine, with one voice. And when the song
fills the night, the mountains and forests are ours.
Now, Cub-of-Mine, the night belongs to you, too.

Let us return down the side of the mountain.

Let us return, Cub-of-Mine.

Come into the snug of the den, Cub-of-Mine.
Come inside and lie down.

Do I have to come in? Do I have to lie down, Papa Wolf?
Where the moon shines bright in the dark of the night –
this is where I belong.

I am big enough now.